AF228601

DOLLY PARTON

REBECCA FELIX

Checkerboard
Library

An Imprint of Abdo Publishing
abdobooks.com

ABDOBOOKS.COM

Published by Abdo Publishing, a division of ABDO, PO Box 398166, Minneapolis, Minnesota 55439.
Copyright © 2022 by Abdo Consulting Group, Inc. International copyrights reserved in all countries.
No part of this book may be reproduced in any form without written permission from the publisher.
Checkerboard Library™ is a trademark and logo of Abdo Publishing.

Printed in the United States of America, North Mankato, Minnesota
052021
092021

Design and Production: Mighty Media, Inc.
Editor: Liz Salzmann
Cover Photograph: JB Lacroix/Getty Images
Interior Photographs: Andrew Harnik/AP Images, pp. 23, 29 (bottom); AP Images, pp. 5, 28 (bottom left); Cherie A. Thurlby/Wikimedia Commons, p. 17; Curt Habraken/AP Images, p. 9; Curtis Hilbun/Wikimedia Commons, pp. 21, 29; Eric Draper/White House/Wikimedia Commons, p. 25; Evan Agostini/AP Images, p. 27; John Mathew Smith/Wikimedia Commons, p. 19; MediaPunch Inc/Alamy, p. 7; Mike Albans/AP Images, p. 15; Moeller Talent/Wikimedia Commons, pp. 13, 28 (top); Seth Poppel/Yearbook Library, pp. 11, 28; Shutterstock Images, p. 17 (paper clip)

Library of Congress Control Number: 2021932875

Publisher's Cataloging-in-Publication Data
Names: Felix, Rebecca, author.
Title: Dolly Parton / by Rebecca Felix
Description: Minneapolis, Minnesota : Abdo Publishing, 2022 | Series: Checkerboard biographies | Includes online resources and index.
Identifiers: ISBN 9781532196027 (lib. bdg.) | ISBN 9781098216887 (ebook)
Subjects: LCSH: Parton, Dolly--Juvenile literature. | Singers--United States--Biography--Juvenile literature. | Women country musicians--United States--Biography--Juvenile literature. | Actors and actresses--Biography--Juvenile literature. | Businesspeople--Biography--Juvenile literature.
Classification: DDC 781.642--dc23

CONTENTS

CHAPTER 1

SUPREME SUPERSTAR

Dolly Parton is one of the most popular celebrities in the world. She became famous as a country singer and songwriter. But she is a successful actor and **producer** too. Parton is also an author, businesswoman, and **philanthropist**.

Parton has numerous music awards and honors. She has more number one hit songs than any other female country artist. Parton is also thought to be one of the most productive, creative songwriters in history.

Parton's philanthropy has helped people in the United States and around the world. She has **donated** more than 100 million books to children. She has also provided relief to families in need and funded medical research.

Parton is known for speaking her mind and having a big heart. Her fans regard Parton as joyful and witty. Parton is beloved around the world. But she began her life dreaming of stardom in a small cabin in the Smoky Mountains of Tennessee.

 **Find out who you are and do it on purpose.** 

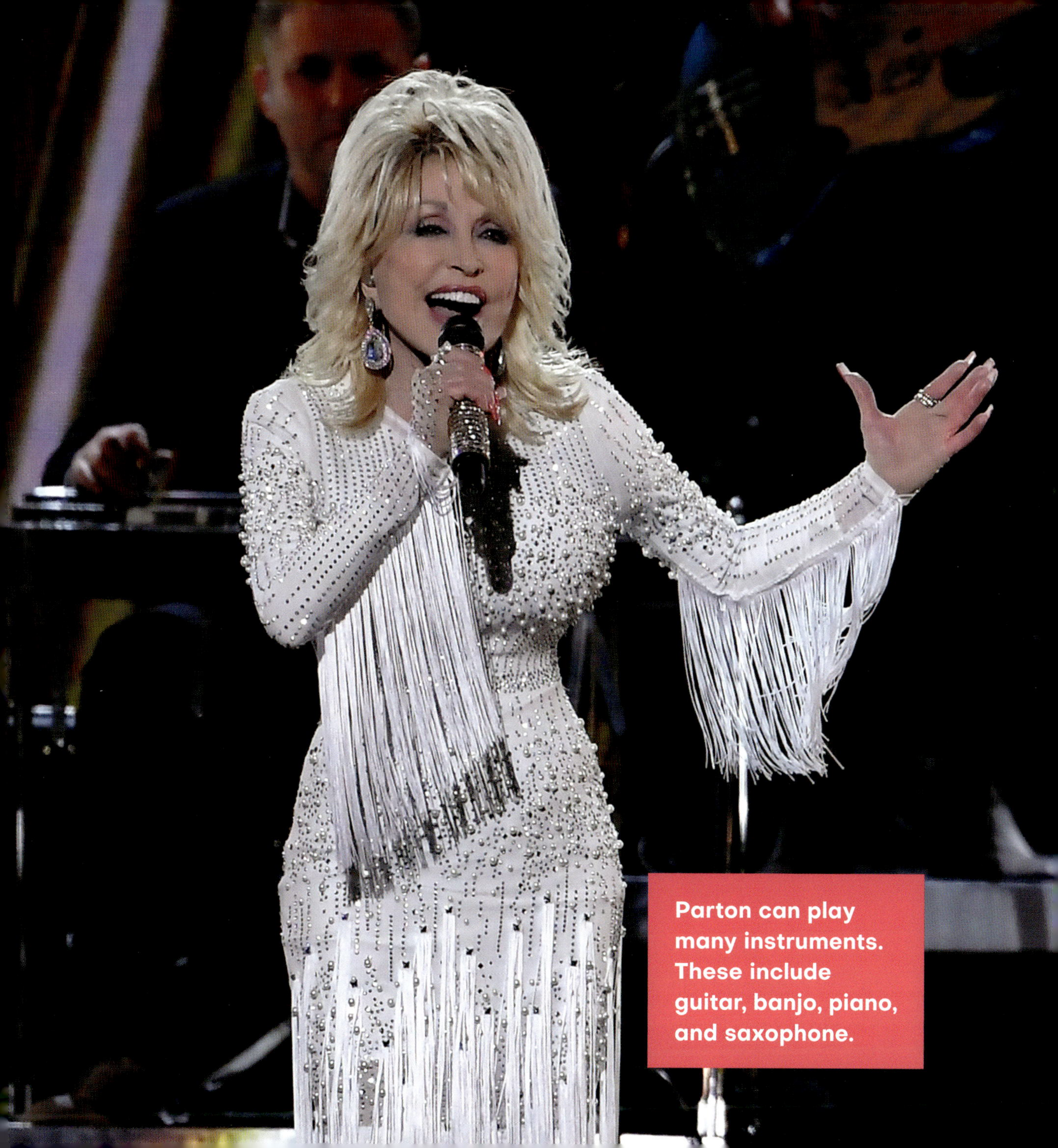

Parton can play
many instruments.
These include
guitar, banjo, piano,
and saxophone.

CHAPTER 2

BORN IN THE BACKWOODS

Dolly Rebecca Parton was born on January 19, 1946, in Locust Ridge, Tennessee. She grew up in the backwoods of nearby Sevierville. Dolly's father, Robert Lee Parton, was a farmer. Dolly's mother, Avie Lee Parton, raised their children.

Dolly had 11 **siblings**. She was born fourth. The entire family lived in a one-room cabin. It did not have electricity or running water.

The Partons didn't have much money to buy the things they needed. So, they got creative. Avie Lee made Dolly a coat out of rags. Dolly also had a doll made from a corncob. It had corn-silk **tassels** for hair.

At age five, Dolly wrote her first song. It was about her doll. She called the song "Little Tiny Tassel Top." At age seven, Dolly made a guitar using spare parts she collected. Dolly practiced playing her homemade guitar. She performed on her front porch, plucking the strings and singing. Dolly dreamed of being a successful singer.

Dolly (*top right*) with her parents (*left*) and siblings in 1960

CHAPTER 3

YOUNG PERFORMER

Dolly wasn't the only member of her family who was passionate about music. Her mother sang. Her grandfather played the fiddle. And her uncle Bill Owens wrote songs.

When Dolly was ten, Owens helped her book professional performances. This included *The Cas Walker Show* in Knoxville, Tennessee. She sang and played guitar on the TV show.

In 1957, when Dolly was 11 years old, she wrote "Puppy Love," with the help of Owens. Dolly recorded the song and Goldband Records released it in 1959, when Dolly was 13.

"Puppy Love" did not make the music charts. But Dolly kept writing songs. The same year, she performed at the world-famous Grand Ole Opry. It is the top country music **venue** in the world. Dolly sang "You Gotta

"COAT OF MANY COLORS"

In 1971, Dolly wrote a song about the coat Avie Lee made her. It is about her real experience of being teased about the shabby coat. But she was proud of the coat because it was made with love. "Coat of Many Colors" became one of Dolly's most famous songs.

Parton and Owens in 2013

Be My Baby." The attendees were very impressed. They requested three **encores** from her that night.

Three years after that first Grand Ole Opry performance, Tree Publishing and Mercury Records signed Dolly and Owens. Dolly recorded her and Owens's songs "It's Sure Gonna Hurt" and "The Love You Give." However, when the songs failed to become hits, the record label dropped the artists.

Dolly began working with a new record label, Somerset, right away. In 1963, she recorded covers of five songs on the album *Hits Made Famous by Country Queens*. The album also included Dolly singing her original song "Letter to Heaven."

Meanwhile, Dolly was also a student. In 1964, she became the first person in her family to graduate from high school. The day after graduation, Dolly boarded a bus to Nashville, Tennessee. The city is considered the world capital of country music. There, Dolly would focus on her dreams full time.

Someone told me later, 'You looked like you were out there saying, "Here I am, this is me."'
(about her 1959 Grand Ole Opry performance)

Parton's senior year photo in her high school yearbook

BIG BREAKS

Parton's first day in Nashville was life changing. She met Carl Thomas Dean while doing laundry at the Wishy Washy Laundromat. The two began dating and married in 1966.

Parton and Owens continued writing songs together. One was "Put It Off Until Tomorrow," written for country singer Bill Phillips. Parton sang backup **vocals**. In 1966, "Put It Off Until Tomorrow" topped the charts! It was also named Broadcast Music, Inc's Song of the Year.

Monument Records took note of Parton's talent. In February 1967, the label released Parton's first album, *Hello, I'm Dolly*. It featured 12 original songs. The opening song, "Dumb Blonde," was a smash. It became Parton's first top-forty hit.

The entire *Hello, I'm Dolly* album was a great success. It caught the attention of Nashville star Porter Wagoner. He hosted *The Porter Wagoner Show*, a popular weekly TV program featuring country music. In September, Wagoner invited Parton to perform on his show.

After a few appearances, Parton was signed on as Wagoner's partner. The show earned her fame across the country. Parton quickly became one of country music's most popular stars.

In 1968, Parton and Wagoner released an album together. *Just Between You and Me* won the Country Music Association (CMA) **Vocal** Group of the Year award.

In the following years, Parton also found **solo** success. In 1971, her song "Joshua" became her first number one hit on the country music charts.

By 1973, Parton had recorded 24 studio albums. Eleven were recorded with Wagoner. The other 13 were solo albums. These albums included 200 songs Parton had written!

Parton kept on writing. That year, she wrote two songs that would become among her most famous. "Jolene" was about a beautiful red-haired woman. "I Will Always Love You," was thought to be a romantic ballad about a couple breaking up. But Parton told the media the song was not romantic.

Parton had decided to leave Wagoner's show and end their professional partnership. She wrote the song about her feelings of thankfulness to Wagoner for their years of working together. Though the song was not about romantic love, it would go on to be one of the top love songs in the world.

2 SONGS, 24 HOURS

Parton wrote and recorded both "Jolene" and "I Will Always Love You" over one 24-hour period! Critics and fans have been in awe of this feat for decades.

Singer and actor Whitney Houston (*right*) recorded "I Will Always Love You" for the 1992 movie *The Bodyguard*. She and producer David Foster (*left*) won Grammy Awards for their version of the song.

CHAPTER 5

COUNTRY & POP

Both "Jolene" and "I Will Always Love You" reached number one on the country music charts in 1974. So did Parton's next three singles! In 1975 and 1976, Parton won the CMA Female **Vocalist** of the Year award. In 1978, Parton was named CMA Entertainer of the Year.

The same year, Parton's album *New Harvest . . . First Gathering* went platinum. This meant it sold at least 1 million copies. Parton was the first female country artist to have a platinum album.

As Parton's success continued to rise, so did her exposure. She went on tour. She performed and gave interviews on many TV programs. She also began to cross over into pop music.

Parton was a music sensation. At the start of the new decade, she stepped into another role. Parton became a movie star.

BLUEGRASS TOO

Parton also recorded successful **bluegrass** albums. In 1999, she released *The Grass Is Blue*. The International Bluegrass Music Association named it Album of the Year. In 2002, Parton's *Little Sparrow* won Best Bluegrass Album from the Association for Independent Music Awards.

BIO BASICS

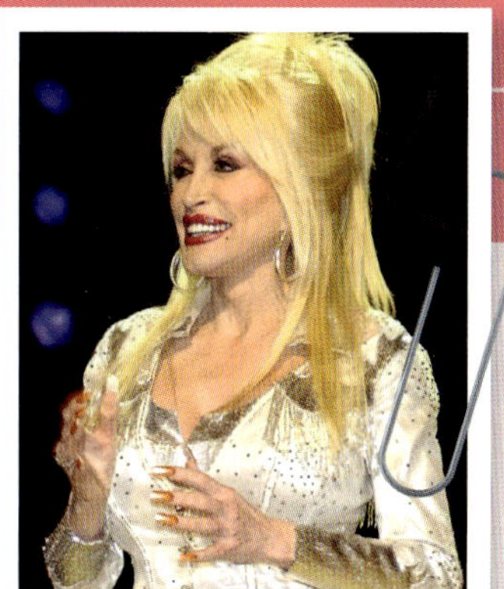

NAME: Dolly Rebecca Parton

NICKNAMES: Aunt Granny, Backwoods Barbie, Book Lady, Iron Butterfly, Leading Lady of Country, Queen of Country, Queen of Nashville, Smoky Mountain Songbird

BIRTH: January 19, 1946, Locust Ridge, Tennessee

SPOUSE: Carl Thomas Dean (1966-present)

FAMOUS FOR: singing, songwriting, acting, and philanthropy

ACHIEVEMENTS: first female country artist to have a platinum album; named CMA Entertainer of the Year in 1978; received a Lifetime Achievement Award at the 2011 Grammy Awards

ONSCREEN SUCCESS

By 1980, Parton's musical talent was recognized around the world. That year, she showed off her acting skills in the movie *9 to 5*. The comedy features three women who work for a **sexist** boss. The women get revenge on their boss for his **inappropriate** behavior. Parton wrote the song "9 to 5" for the film. It reached number one on both the pop and country music charts.

Parton earned three Golden Globe Award nominations for the film. These were Best Actress in a Motion Picture Musical or Comedy, New Star of the Year (Actress), and Best Song in a Motion Picture.

The song "9 to 5" earned Parton additional honors. It won Best Country Song and Best Country **Vocal** Performance by a Female at that year's Grammy Awards. Parton was also named the Academy of Country Music Female Vocalist of the Year.

SANDOLLAR PRODUCTIONS

In 1986, Parton cofounded Sandollar Productions. The company **produced** the 1992 movie *Buffy the Vampire Slayer*. Sandollar also produced the popular TV show of the same name from 1997 to 2003.

Parton went on to star in several more major films. She also acted in several made-for-TV movies and appeared as a guest star on many TV shows. By the mid-1980s, Parton's onscreen success was far from over. But she turned her focus to yet another calling.

CHAPTER 7

CHARITABLE TRAILBLAZER

In 1986, Parton became the owner of an amusement park in Pigeon Forge, Tennessee. Parton and her business partners renamed the park Dollywood. It has rides, crafts, and musical events.

The park is also home to the Southern Gospel Museum and Hall of Fame. Dollywood became one of the top tourist attractions in the South. Its revenue helped the economy and provided jobs in Parton's home county of Sevier.

Two years after Dollywood opened, Parton established the Dollywood Foundation. Her goal for the foundation was to reduce high school dropout rates in Sevier County. The Buddy Program was one part

EAGLE PRESERVATION

Parton opened Eagle Mountain **Sanctuary** at Dollywood in 1991. The sanctuary is home to bald eagles that cannot live in the wild. In 2003, the US Fish & Wildlife Service awarded Parton its Partnership Award for her work to preserve the species.

In 2010, Dollywood received the Liseberg Applause Award. This is a Swedish award for the most inspiring and creative theme parks.

of the foundation. Parton asked students to pair up and encourage each other to do well in school. Parton then gave each Buddy Program student $500 if they graduated. In 1989, Parton also gave $500 to every Sevier County high school graduate who attended nearby Hiwassee College.

In 1995, the Dollywood Foundation began the Imagination Library. American children who are signed up for the program receive one free book each month from birth to age five. In later years, the program expanded to Canada, the United Kingdom, Australia, and Ireland. By 2018, the Imagination Library had **donated** more than 100 million books to children!

Parton's passion for supporting education continued. In 2000, she established the Dolly Parton **Scholarship**. Every year, it gives $15,000 each to five Sevier County graduates to spend on a college education.

Parton has supported Tennesseans after natural **disasters** as well. In 2016, she founded the My People Fund. It provided nearly $9 million to people affected by that year's Smoky Mountains wildfires.

In 2018, Parton spoke at the US Library of Congress in Washington, DC. The event was in honor of the Imagination Library's 100 millionth book donation.

Health care is another of Parton's charitable passions. She has **donated** millions of dollars to build hospitals and fund research. In 2020, Parton gave $1 million to the drug company Moderna. This donation helped fund its successful vaccine for the **COVID-19** disease that had caused a **pandemic**.

CHAPTER 8

CULTURAL ICON

While working on her many charities, Parton continued to act, sing, and write songs. In 1994, she added author to her list of accomplishments. Her **autobiography** *Dolly: My Life and Other Unfinished Business* became a bestseller. It would be one of many books Parton wrote during her lifetime.

Parton's lifelong success has been honored by many musical institutions. But Parton has also earned recognition for her positive influence. In 2004, she was given the US Library of Congress Living Legend Award. This honored Parton's contributions to the country's **cultural** and social **heritage**.

Country music was forever changed by Parton. She is credited with giving it a wider appeal. And before Parton's career began, men dominated the country music industry. Parton was one of several female artists who led the way for future generations.

Parton's upbringing was also inspirational. Her rise to fame is often called a "rags-to-riches" story. Many people identified with the financial struggles Parton

US president George W. Bush (*center*) and First Lady Laura Bush (*third from right*) with the 2006 Kennedy Center Honors recipients, including Parton

> " I don't feel I have to march, hold up a sign or label myself. I think the way I have conducted my life and my business and myself speaks for itself. "

experienced in childhood. This helped many people relate to her.

Fans also admire Parton's straightforward, genuine nature. She is known for speaking her mind when she feels the need to. But her influence is often unspoken. The way Parton lives her life inspires many people. She displays a positive attitude, **self-confidence**, and kindness.

Researchers have examined Parton's **cultural** influence in books, interviews, and shows. The study of her life is also a college course at the University of Tennessee! The course is called Dolly's America.

Parton has been a star for more than 50 years. She has recorded 25 number one songs and has had 41 albums rank in the top ten in country music. Parton transformed the music industry, inspired millions of people, and shaped American culture. Whatever Parton pursues next is sure to be as extraordinary as her past.

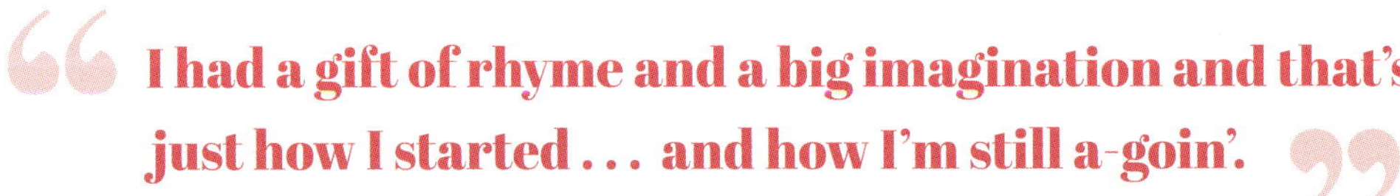

In 2016, Parton received the Willie Nelson Lifetime Achievement Award from the CMA.

TIMELINE

1946

Dolly Rebecca Parton is born on January 19 in Locust Ridge, Tennessee.

1959

Dolly performs at the Grand Ole Opry.

1967

Parton releases her first album, *Hello, I'm Dolly*. She becomes Porter Wagoner's cohost on his country music TV show.

1980

Parton appears in the movie *9 to 5*.

1951

Dolly writes her first song, "Little Tiny Tassel Top."

1964

Dolly graduates from high school and moves to Nashville, Tennessee.

1971

Parton's song "Joshua" becomes her first number one hit on the country charts.

1986

Parton opens Dollywood.

1994

Dolly: My Life and Other Unfinished Business is published.

2004

Parton earns the Living Legend Award from the US Library of Congress.

2020

Parton donates $1 million to help develop a COVID-19 vaccine.

1988

Parton founds the Dollywood Foundation.

1995

The Dollywood Foundation establishes the Imagination Library.

autobiography—a story of a person's life that is written by himself or herself.

bluegrass—a type of traditional American music that is played on stringed instruments, such as banjos and fiddles.

COVID-19—a serious illness that first appeared in late 2019.

cultural—of or relating to the customs, arts, and tools of a nation or a people at a certain time.

disaster—an event that causes damage, destruction, and often loss of life.

donate—to give. A donation is something that is donated.

encore—a demand by an audience for a performance to continue or be repeated.

heritage—something handed down from one generation to the next.

inappropriate—not suitable, fitting, or proper.

pandemic—an outbreak of a disease that spreads quickly throughout the world.

philanthropist—a person who shows a spirit of goodwill toward all people, especially through generosity and charity. A philanthropist's act is philanthropy.

produce—to oversee or provide money for a play, TV show, movie, or album.

sanctuary—a refuge for wildlife where predators are controlled and hunting is illegal.

scholarship—money or aid given to help a student continue his or her studies.

self-confidence—faith in oneself and one's powers.

sexist—related to the unfair treatment of people because of their sex.

sibling—a brother or a sister.

solo—a performance by a single person.

tassel—a flower or group of flowers at the top of a cornstalk.

venue—the building or location where an event takes place.

vocals—the parts of a song performed by the human voice. Someone who sings a song is a vocalist.

ONLINE RESOURCES

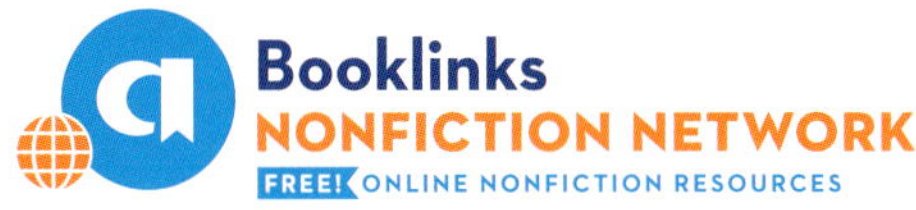

To learn more about Dolly Parton, please visit **abdobooklinks.com** or scan this QR code. These links are routinely monitored and updated to provide the most current information available.

INDEX